Past Loves

A play in one-act by Martin Lindsay

Moody Lapcat Books

First paperback edition in 2023.

Design and Cover by Martin Lindsay.

Images by Martin Lindsay and Canva.

ISBN: 978-0-6451987-5-1 (paperback)

ISBN: 978-0-6451987-4-4 (ebook)

Published by Moody Lapcat Books

Perth, Western Australia

www.moodylapcatbooks.com

contact@moodylapcatbooks.com

Performing rights

Any performance or public reading of Past Loves is forbidden unless a licence has been received from the author or the author's agent. The purchase of this book in no way gives the purchaser the right to perform the play in public, whether by the means of a staged production or a reading.

All applications for public performance should be directed to the playwright c/- Moody Lapcat Books.

Copying for educational purposes

The Australian Copyright Act 1968 (Act) allows a maximum of one chapter or 10% of this book, whichever is the greater, to be reproduced and/or communicated by any educational institution for its educational purposes provided that educational institution or the body that administers it) has given a remuneration notice to Copyright Agency Limited (CAL) under the Act.

For details of the CAL license for educational institutions contact CAL, Level 15, 233 Castlereagh Street, Sydney NSW 2000. Tel: (02) 9394 7600; email: info@copyright.com.au.

Copying for other purposes

Except as permitted under the Act, for example a fair dealing for the purposes of study, research, criticism or review, all rights are reserved. This publication (or any part of it) may not be reproduced or transmitted, copied, stored, distributed or otherwise made available by any person or entity (including Google, Amazon or similar organisations), in any form (electronic, digital, optical, mechanical) or by any means

Characters

BEN – 20s to 50s

"There is a very big difference between infidelity and a quick hand-shandy to a saucy website."

Easy-going and loyal, Ben's conflict avoidance and accommodating nature has – till now – kept the peace.

ANGIE – 20s to 50s

"Rationality means nothing when the heart knows what's clearly true."

Confident in her various interests and beliefs, Angela runs a strict house with no time for others' nonsense.

RICHARD – 20s to 50s

"Well, I'm going to confront her about it. Force her to own up. And whoever it is, I'll smash the bastard."

Alpha male with the boys, less so at home, Richard has no anger issues and will deck anyone who suggests so.

DONNA – 20s to 50s

"So how do we do this? Sit round a campfire with our feet in hummus chanting "Omm" until you finally apologise?"

In contrast to partner Ben, Donna is direct, assertive and all too happy to resort to sarcasm.

WAITRESS/BARMAID/TESS – 20s to 40s

Three different people or alternate lives existing in parallel?

"Sounds like it's not the first time you've made a little mess."

> The Waitress is insanely curious when there's a bit of
> gossip to be overheard.

"Like I've never heard that one a million times before."

> The Barmaid is sick of your crap, whatever it may be.

*"I'm simply a facilitator, allowing my clients to experience the full extent
of all life experiences."*

> Tess the therapist is serenely calm and polite, assured in
> her abilities.

Settings

Scene 1 – Café

Consists of a counter with props, two tables with two chairs and appropriate dressing.

Scene 2 – Bar

Consists of a counter with props and two bar stools.

Scene 3 – Suburban living room

Consists of a "fireplace" with mantelpiece props.

Scene 4 – Café

As before, but with only one table with two chairs.

Production Notes

To assist swift scene changes:

- The Café COUNTER becomes a BAR by removing the COFFEE MACHINE and ITEMS, and then adding BAR TAPS. The STOOLS remain.

- The BAR becomes a MANTELPIECE by removal of the BAR TAPS and STOOLS, with ORNAMENTS and a FIRE GUARD.

- The MANTELPIECE becomes a Café COUNTER by removal of ORNAMENTS and FIRE GUARD, and return the STOOLS, COFFEE MACHINE and ITEMS.

For WAITRESS/BARMAID/TESS quick changes:

- WAITRESS wears an APRON over blacks.

- Removes APRON, slings TEA TOWEL over shoulder as BARMAID.

- Removes TEA TOWEL to don BUSINESS JACKET and PANTS.

- Removes BUSINESS JACKET and PANTS to put on APRON to become WAITRESS again.

Café "STEAMER" is some sort of concealed device to produce a spurt of "steam" from behind the COFFEE MACHINE on cue.

First Performed

Old Mill Theatre, Perth, Western Australia, 2010.

Directed by Jeff Watkins.

Original Cast

- Ben – Murray Jackson.

- Angie – Anna Peluso.

- Richard – Martin Lindsay.

- Donna – Lisa Skrypichayko.

- Waitress/Barmaid/Tess – Grace Edwards.

Winner of the 2010 Southwest Drama Festival Best Play.

Winner of the 2010 Southwest Drama Festival Best Script.

We are not the same persons this year as last; nor are those we love.

W. Somerset Maugham

Past Loves

SCENE ONE – CAFÉ

WAITRESS tends to COFFEES at COUNTER, behind a COFFEE MACHINE. The COUNTER has a BOWL OF MUFFINS displayed for sale.

ANGIE sits at TABLE, waiting impatiently. She checks her WATCH, unimpressed.

SOUND FX: Angry car honk in traffic.

BEN

(*Off, distant*) Shit! Sorry!

Recognising BEN's voice, ANGIE rolls her eyes.

SOUND FX: Tinkle of shop-door BELL.

BEN rushes in and looks around the shop.

ANGIE waves, catching his attention.

BEN crosses to her, making a bit much of his pretend breathlessness by leaning on CHAIR.

BEN

Sorry Ange. Could barely get out the door at work.

ANGIE

(Dubious) I see.

BEN

And then there was this … thing I had to do before leaving.

ANGIE

Fine.

BEN

And traffic is absolutely crazy. *(Indicates back to "WINDOW")* … Obviously it's died down a bit now, but a few minutes ago – crazy.

ANGIE

I rarely expect you on time anyway, Ben. So, if you've finished with your list of prepared excuses, will you please sit down.

BEN hovers, unwilling to concede she has called him out precisely.

BEN

… parking was a bit shit, too.

ANGIE gives withering look.

A beat, then BEN obediently sits, then springs back up.

BEN

I'll just order a -…

ANGIE

I ordered for you. Flat white, two sugars.

BEN

Oh! You're a mind reader. *(Joking)* Or are you this week? … Sorry, no offence.

ANGIE *gives impatient nod for him to sit.* BEN *sits.*

BEN

So, how are you? Sorry for keeping your hubby out last weekend. How did Richard pull up on Sunday?

ANGIE

Fine. We're both fine.

BEN

Good. Donna and I are too.

ANGIE

(Mind elsewhere) … are two what? Oh. Yes, good. Look, Ben, I've asked you to coffee for a reason.

BEN

Yeah, I thought there must be.

ANGIE *is immediately interested.*

ANGIE

Did you? Did you … *sense* something?

BEN

No, I just sort of thought "I'm the last person Angie would invite to coffee". Or anything, really.

ANGIE

Not the *very* last, Benjamin.

BEN nods acknowledgement of this small concession.

ANGIE

So, you must understand I've asked you here for something very important.

BEN

(Worried) Richard didn't tell you what I said about your crystal healing classes, did he?

ANGIE

No, this is- … What did you say about my crystal healing classes?

BEN

Nothing whatsoever. And he probably misheard it anyway.

ANGIE eyes BEN in suspicion, then bows head, consumed by worry.

BEN

Is there something wrong?

ANGIE

There is. Very much so. *(Deep breath)* Ben, … I've had an affair.

BEN is stunned.

Without looking up, WAITRESS leans sideways so as to eavesdrop.

BEN checks if anyone is listening as ANGIE dabs her eyes with NAPKIN to maintain composure.

BEN leans forward to speak privately.

BEN

An affair? How? Why? ... How?

ANGIE

It happened before I could stop it. If I'd only known where things would go ...

BEN

Where did things go?

ANGIE

Where do you think things went!

BEN looks around, hoping ANGIE's raised voice hasn't attracted attention. He leans forward again.

BEN

What, all the way...?

ANGIE holds NAPKIN to mouth, ashamed to speak, then nods.

BEN flounders for words.

BEN

Does Richard know?

ANGIE shakes her head.

BEN

You're going to tell him, surely?

ANGIE

I have no choice.

BEN

I mean, you have to. He's my best mate, so obviously I insist. God, he'll be shattered.

ANGIE

You don't think I know that? My whole marriage is at risk. But I can't not tell him.

BEN

You've told no one else?

ANGIE

No one knows Richard better than you.

WAITRESS delivers two COFFEES, pretending all is fine.

Drinks served, WAITRESS loiters.

BEN and ANGIE wait impatiently for her to depart.

WAITRESS returns to innocently wipe down COUNTER, but

clearly listening in.

BEN

May I ask who with?

ANGIE summons herself to speak.

ANGIE

You.

BEN halts, stunned.

WAITRESS coughs impatiently, prompting him.

BEN comes to.

BEN

But we haven't - … have we? *(Thinks, just in case)*
No. We couldn't have. That I remember. Did we?

ANGIE

Not here and now, obviously. I'm not exact, but I
think sometime in 1852. About September.

BEN

… 1852?

ANGIE

Thereabouts. It's difficult to exactly place a past
life experience.

BEN

Past life? *(Relieved)* Oh, I thought you were serious for a minute there.

ANGIE

I'm completely serious, Ben.

BEN

You can't be, surely.

ANGIE

I hope you're not mocking my beliefs.

BEN is immediately defensive, having been on the receiving end of ANGIE's wrath before.

BEN

Of course not. As you yourself have said … quite a number of times … who's to say what anyone believes is or isn't valid. But, to suggest something like- …

ANGIE

I'm not suggesting. We were lovers in a past life.

BEN

We were?

ANGIE

We *were*.

BEN

You and me …

BEN *looks round for eavesdroppers. WAITRESS wipes COUNTER with more gusto.*

BEN

… were *lovers.*

ANGIE

Yes!

As conversation proceeds, WAITRESS polishes anything on COUNTER to remain within earshot – SPOON, FORK, MUFFINS.

BEN

Who told you this?

ANGIE

I found out myself. In a session with my therapist. We were exploring an emotional blockage stemming from a previous existential conflict.

BEN

Sounds nasty.

ANGIE

It is. An unresolved issue from a past life has huge consequences if left unaddressed.

BEN

Does it.

ANGIE

Given the intensity of this blockage, she suggested regression hypnotherapy. But it turned out a disaster.

BEN

Should've called a plumber?

ANGIE

You don't know what regression hypnotherapy is, do you?

BEN

Not a clue.

ANGIE

It's a journey into a deep hypnotic state in order to relive a previous experience as though it were currently happening.

BEN

And you pay someone *money* for this?

ANGIE

The money is immaterial.

BEN

That's not what Richard says.

ANGIE

I regressed back to the moment of blockage. The blockage was you.

BEN

I've been called worse.

WAITRESS now innocently polishes front of COUNTER then moves to polish nearest TABLE.

ANGIE

We were forbidden lovers. You a farmhand, me the farmer's daughter promised to another.

BEN

To another farmer's daughter?

ANGIE

No, that would be ridiculous in 1852.

BEN

Clearly ridiculous.

ANGIE

But we didn't take the situation lying down. So to speak. We consummated our love, secretly, one night in the barn.

BEN

I get hay fever.

ANGIE

Not in your previous life, you didn't.

BEN

How are you so sure it was me?

ANGIE

I could tell by your aura. They remain constant across all our lives. Lingering around you as an eternal presence.

BEN

A bit like cheap deodorant, then?

ANGIE

A bit like *your* deodorant, yes.

BEN gives his armpit a quick self-conscious sniff.

BEN

So, what … we *did it?* In a barn. In a past life.

ANGIE

(*Folds arms adamantly*) Yes.

BEN

… Was I any good?

Noticing WAITRESS polishing in earshot, ANGIE coughs.

Caught, WAITRESS immediately goes into service mode.

WAITRESS

Everything okay?

BEN

Fine. Fine. We once did it in a barn, you know.

WAITRESS

Oh, really. *(Points at their COFFEES)* Fancy
another round?

BEN

I doubt the farmer would be too happy if we did.

WAITRESS

(Farmer voice) "You can go sow your oats
elsewhere" he'd say.

BEN and ANGIE stare at WAITRESS.

WAITRESS gently clears her throat.

WAITRESS

Whoever or whatever you're talking about.

WAITRESS hurries back behind COUNTER to look busy.

ANGIE

This isn't funny, Ben. We've cheated on Richard.

BEN

No, we haven't. If – and it's a pretty dodgy if – *if*
there is such a thing as past lives, then so what?
It was 1852. At very worst, I'm just an old flame.

ANGIE

Regression hypnotherapy is a re-experiencing of
a past event. You relive it as though it was
happening at that very moment. As far as I'm

concerned, we had sex last week.

WAITRESS

Awkward.

They look to WAITRESS, who pretends to struggle with the COFFEE MACHINE.

WAITRESS

(Struggling) Awkward bloody thing.

BEN

In your head, we did.

ANGIE

I wilfully had sex with someone besides Richard. I've been unfaithful!

BEN

Not physically!

ANGIE

Emotionally!

BEN

Well, that hardly matters.

ANGIE

That's everything! Physical betrayal is one thing, but this was emotional infidelity.

BEN

Subconsciously.

ANGIE

I was fully awake and aware the entire time.

BEN

It means nothing! It's just fantasy.

ANGIE

With respect, Benjamin, I do not fantasise about you.

BEN

I mean, a mental image of some real or imagined person. There's no one there. Nothing actually happens. It's like … picturing yourself in your own naughty adult movie. Like those point-of-view ones you come across online.

ANGIE

I certainly don't come across them.

BEN

…I read an article about them. And how daydreaming imaginary scenarios is a perfectly healthy tension release that hurts no one.

ANGIE

Imagining yourself with someone other than your partner is cheating.

BEN

No, it's not.

ANGIE

Of course it is.

BEN

There is a very big difference between infidelity and a quick hand-shandy to a saucy website. Otherwise, buying a box of tissues would be admissible as bigamy.

ANGIE

You seem to know a lot about these saucy websites.

BEN

… It was a very detailed article. All I'm trying to say is that a bit of escapist fantasy is not cheating.

ANGIE

It is if you emotionally commit to it.

BEN unleashes his secret weapon.

BEN

Mr Darcy … in a wet shirt … in the pond.

ANGIE visibly reacts with a case of the wibbles.

WAITRESS accidentally engages the STEAMER on the COFFEE MACHINE. Steam billows up.

Both women quickly compose themselves.

ANGIE

What about him?

BEN

You went gooey!

ANGIE

I did not!

BEN

You bloody well did.

ANGIE

Only over Jane Austen's beautiful prose. Anyway, that's just books and tv or movies, designed to make you think things.

BEN

And that's exactly what's happening in this past life regression of yours. Some random mental image popping into your head that you just go with it. It's a fantasy that never happened to you. Just like my example.

ANGIE

Your example being thinking about of people while masturbating to pornography?

WAITRESS drops SPOON in surprise.

BEN and ANGIE look to WAITRESS.

WAITRESS

Sorry.

BEN leans forward in damage control, fearing everyone is listening.

BEN

Not me! But if I did – which I don't – then maybe occasionally I might harmlessly imagine what it was like with someone else.

ANGIE

God, you're like a serial cheater!

BEN

If I did. Which I don't. I'm just being hypothetical.

ANGIE

You're being immoral.

BEN

It's just natural human curiosity, to occasionally daydream about other people we encounter – or will never encounter. And sort of explore where it might end up.

ANGIE

I think I know where it all ends up.

BEN

It's just a harmless, healthy outlet with a figment of your imagination.

ANGIE

So, you won't mind me mentioning all this to
Donna.

BEN

Don't you dare!

ANGIE

So, "harmless and healthy" is it?

WAITRESS interrupts to gather their CUPS.

WAITRESS

Anything else? Coffee? Cake? Haybale?

BEN

(Frowns) No, thank you.

*WAITRESS returns to COUNTER. BEN sulkily sips COFFEE
as ANGIE straightens for an announcement.*

ANGIE

I have to tell Richard we've been unfaithful.

*BEN spits out coffee. WAITRESS rushes over to mop floor with
WASHCLOTH.*

BEN

I'm so sorry!

WAITRESS

Never mind. Sounds like it's not the first time

you've made a little mess.

BEN leans to ANGIE, keeping voice down.

BEN

Are you freaking nuts?

ANGIE

Last week I freshly experienced us making love. I can't be in a relationship based on deception. Richard must know.

BEN

You … me … we have not been unfaithful. On the sliding scale of infidelity, it does not register.

BEN mimes an imaginary line before himself, moving nearest hand as a boundary towards ANGIE.

BEN

At this end: Having physical relations. Red zone, game over. We both agree, this is infidelity.

ANGIE nods. BEN edges other hand along, away from TABLE.

BEN

Moving back a bit … a brainless drunken snog at pub closing time. Lip contact. Possibly tongues. Cheating?

WAITRESS

How drunk?

BEN

Does it matter?

WAITRESS

Lights come up and you're kissing Quasimodo
then you're probably too pissed for it to count.

ANGIE

I think I will have another coffee, thank you.

*Taking the hint, WAITRESS returns to COUNTER to make the
coffee, still eavesdropping.*

BEN

Okay, so – drunken snog. Bad but saveable?

ANGIE

Cheating.

BEN shrugs at her rigidity, then moves hand further along.

BEN

Further along, a stray lingering gaze at someone
when your partner isn't looking. Or worse, *is*
looking.

ANGIE

Cheating.

BEN

For just looking? Surely, it's simply just
appreciation. Like window shopping for a pair of
shoes you'll never have.

ANGIE

There is no "never" when it comes to shoes. Just persistence. That's why looking is wrong.

BEN

Okay, bad analogy. *(Moving hand further away)* Moving on, walking hand in hand along a lovely beach with sunbathers in bikinis and speedos.

ANGIE

Are you wearing sunglasses?

BEN

Probably.

ANGIE

Cheating.

BEN

(Moves hand further away) Further along – Idle, saucy daydreams?

ANGIE

How idle? How saucy?

BEN

You tell me, Miss Elizabeth Bennet.

ANGIE

(Wavering) That's probably okay. It's imaginary.

BEN *moves hands further away from table.*

BEN

Dreaming of your favourite celebrity.

ANGIE

Of course not. It'll never happen.

BEN now reaching away from table.

BEN

Happening upon a photo of some old boyfriend and remembering a happy time with them.

ANGIE

No. That's just history.

BEN

Bringing us to, relatively speaking …

BEN stands then moves towards DOOR.

BEN

Way, way over here, if not actually across the road and down to the post office: Totally imaginary, historical, never-going-to-or-have-happened past life experiences under the influence of new age mumbo jumbo.

ANGIE stares at him, unimpressed.

ANGIE

Cheating.

BEN

But that's totally irrational.

ANGIE

Rationality means nothing when the heart knows what's clearly true.

BEN notices WAITRESS watching, shaking CHOCOLATE SHAKER on coffees. She shrugs back at him.

BEN returns to his seat, exhausted. WAITRESS continues shaking "chocolate" absent-mindedly, listening intently.

ANGIE

Richard needs to know.

BEN winces.

ANGIE

And you have to tell him.

BEN

Like hell!

ANGIE

You're his best friend.

BEN

Not for much longer if I do!

ANGIE

Maybe your blockage from a past life is not

facing up to responsibility.

BEN

I do not have any blockages!

WAITRESS

You obviously haven't tried the carrot cake.

They look to her. WAITRESS shrugs innocently.

As they continue, WAITRESS attempts to brush off the mountain of "chocolate" she's sprinkled on the COFFEEs.

BEN

Angie, please see sense. Past life regression is nonsense. It's make-believe.

ANGIE

You said you respected my beliefs.

BEN

I was just being patronising. I could hardly tell my best friend that his partner is a fruit loop.

ANGIE

Your previous self would never say something like that. You've obviously devolved.

BEN

Look, what you experienced last week-

ANGIE

And yesterday.

BEN

You went back?

ANGIE

I had to be sure. *(Gooey)* It was by a river that time.

WAITRESS arrives with COFFEEs.

WAITRESS

Ooh, very romantic.

BEN and ANGIE glower at WAITRESS. WAITRESS serves COFFEEs then returns to COUNTER.

ANGIE brushes away excess "chocolate" from her COFFEE.

BEN

We had sex more than once?

ANGIE

We couldn't get enough! *(Regains composure)* And that's why Richard has to know. I have feelings for someone else.

BEN

Who doesn't exist.

ANGIE

Who *did* exist. And part of him still does, in you. That's probably why you always know what to get me for my birthday.

BEN *rubs face with hands.*

ANGIE

The blockage of that relationship hampers my openness with Richard until we face up to it. My therapist explained it all.

BEN

Alright. I'll tell Richard. If only to state how bat-shit insane this whole thing is before you do.

ANGIE pats his arm, BEN shies at the contact.

ANGIE

It's for the best.

They sit, a tense silence over them.

ANGIE

Your previous self would treat for the coffees.

BEN

Don't push it.

LIGHTS down.

SCENE TWO – BAR

The Café COUNTER has been transformed into a BAR with TAPS and STOOL in front.

LIGHTS UP

RICHARD stands with PINT, sternly surveying the crowd around him, itching for a confrontation.

BEN turns from BAR with a fresh PINT, returning CREDIT CARD into a pocket.

He wilts on seeing RICHARD, still to broach the topic. He hesitantly chinks RICHARD's PINT with his own, with a pretence of carefree bonhomie.

BEN

Cheers!

Woken from troubled thoughts, RICHARD regards their drinks then nods without enthusiasm.

BEN sips his PINT, psyching up.

BEN makes to speak, hesitates, then braces himself.

BEN

Rich.

RICHARD

Yeah?

BEN immediately chickens out.

BEN

… How's your drink?

RICHARD

(Looks at PINT) Not much different from the last time you asked.

BEN nods, shrinking back. Annoyed at himself, he tries again.

BEN

Look, Rich.

RICHARD turns, BEN freezes.

BEN

… Bloody good game the other night.

RICHARD

Which one?

BEN

Any of them.

RICHARD

Didn't see. Good, was it?

BEN

I don't know, I didn't see it either.

RICHARD grabs a BAR MAT and begins tearing pieces, eying the surrounding crowd.

BEN girds for another try when RICHARD suddenly cracks.

RICHARD

Mate. I think Angie's having an affair.

BEN chokes in surprise.

BEN

Drink went down the wrong way. *(Hides full glass)* Nah mate, Angie wouldn't do that.

RICHARD

You reckon?

BEN

Definitely not. Absolutely, no. In any way, physical or otherwise.

RICHARD

Otherwise?

BEN

Otherwise, you'd get really upset.

RICHARD

Upset? I'm bloody livid, mate.

RICHARD scowls, tearing at BAR MAT.

BEN

What makes you think…?

RICHARD

Just … things. Little changes and differences.
Stuff like that.

BEN

Just your imagination. And speaking of imaginary
nonsense-…

RICHARD

It's not nonsense, mate. I read this article about
it. "Top Ten Signs Your Partner is Cheating".
And she's showing at least six of them.

BEN

You can't believe those things. They put ideas in
your head, see stuff that isn't there. And speaking
of silly ideas in someone's head-…

RICHARD

Sign number one: Your partner becomes
noticeably more withdrawn, or noticeably more
out-going.

BEN

Which one's the sign?

RICHARD

Either. Both. It's about noticeable change from

normal.

BEN

It's bound to be noticeable if you're looking to notice it.

RICHARD

Well, it's hard not to notice things of late. Like number two. A sudden new consuming interest their partner isn't a part of.

BEN

Ange has always hated all your footy training sessions.

RICHARD

Not me. Her! With this hypno-hydrotherapy thing she's started.

BEN freezes.

RICHARD

And why she's going along to it so much.

BEN

A couple of times.

BEN reacts, trying to shush his knowledge.

RICHARD

Four times this week, mate!

BEN

(*Nearly spills PINT*) *Four* times?

RICHARD

It's like she can't get enough of it.

BEN swigs back a large gulp from PINT.

RICHARD

And each time she comes back all relaxed, with this calm look on her face.

BEN nods then has another gulp.

RICHARD

Like she has no troubles in the world.

BEN

It's probably relaxing. Like meditating. Dreaming up all sorts of silly, unbelievable things that could never *ever* happen.

RICHARD

Yeah? Well, I wonder if there's more to these hypno-hydro-whatever sessions. Like, they're actually when she's seeing someone else. A plumber, maybe.

BEN

Definitely not. Anyone – *anything* she does see is purely imagination.

RICHARD

Well, I'm going to confront her about it. Force
her to own up. And whoever it is, I'll smash the
bastard.

*BEN hides from RICHARD's ire with a large gulp of his drink, then
placing PINT on BAR.*

BAR MAID enters, TOWEL on shoulder. She lifts BEN's PINT.

BAR MAID

Another one?

BEN recognises BARMAID but can't place where.

BEN

What? Oh. No, thanks. Excuse me, but have we
met somewhere before?

BAR MAID

Like I've never heard that one a million times
before.

BAR MAID notices BAR MAT pieces on floor.

BAR MAID

Oi!

BAR MAID flicks TOWEL at RICHARD. He stops, guilty.

BAR MAID departs. BEN is confused but remembers the situation.

BEN

Come on, Rich. As if Angie would cheat on a big old hunk like you. She's probably more worried about women flinging themselves at you.

RICHARD

Sign number three. They make weak jokes about cheating.

BEN

Of course, it's no laughing matter.

RICHARD

Sign number four. Carrying their mobile with them at every moment.

BEN

Who doesn't?

RICHARD

Hiding all messages and callers?

BEN

Maybe she's organising a surprise party for you.

RICHARD

What for?

BEN

… That would spoil the surprise.

RICHARD dissects another BAR MAT.

RICHARD

Sign five. They suddenly start buying you flowers.

BEN

Angie's buying you flowers?

RICHARD

The place is full of them.

BEN

Yeah, for the house, not for you.

RICHARD

She also bought me chocolates. She ate them all, admittedly, but suspicious all the same.

BEN

It's nothing!

RICHARD

Sign number six. Constantly running late or missing things.

BEN

Isn't Angie often late?

RICHARD

Yes, but is she currently late for a *reason*?

BEN

How would you know?

RICHARD

Exactly. Sign number eight.

BEN

What happened to seven?

RICHARD

Seven was "Developing noticeably agitated sub-conscious habits".

RICHARD and BEN look at BAR MAT pieces in his hand. RICHARD drops them.

RICHARD

Angie's not showing any of them.

BAR MAID enters with BROOM. She glares at RICHARD, then aggressively sweeps BAR MAT pieces OFF, making RICHARD jump out of her way.

BEN is sure he recognises her.

RICHARD

Sign number eight.

Startled, BEN composes himself again.

RICHARD

The guilty cheater often confides in a close friend, who then acts strange about you.

BEN sits nervously on BAR STOOL, hunched, legs crossed, covering mouth.

BEN

No idea about that. At all. Nothing.

RICHARD

Sign nine. Nervous body language. Covering the mouth, defensive crossing of legs, mumbling, unable to keep eye contact, hunched.

BEN uncovers, uncrosses, then unhunches as they're mentioned, nearly falling off BAR STOOL.

RICHARD

Then there's the last sign. Sometimes they show no signs at all. They're that good at covering up.

BEN

You sure this article wasn't "Top Ten Ways to Convince a Partner You're a Paranoid Nutjob"?

RICHARD

You think I'm imagining it?

BEN

I think everyone is imagining things. You don't want to get all angry and jump to conclusions. Like that footy final when you got reported for striking.

RICHARD

That was just a little love-tap.

BEN

He was the umpire, Rich. All I'm saying is maybe
we should be careful about over-active
imaginations before things get out of hand.

RICHARD

Maybe. But if I'm right, heaven help whoever it
is, because I'm going to kill him.

BEN signals for another drink, urgently.

SCENE THREE – LIVING ROOM

The Pub BAR is transformed into a draped MANTELPIECE with FRAMED PICTURES and ORNAMENTS with a FIREPLACE GUARD in front.

LIGHTS UP.

ANGIE arranges ORNAMENTS in preparation for company.

SOUND FX: A doorbell.

ANGIE checks WATCH then hurries OFF to "Front door".

ANGIE leads in a very unimpressed DONNA in a COAT.

ANGIE

Do come on through. I hope the place isn't too much of a mess.

DONNA

No. Only the situation.

ANGIE

Can I take your coat?

DONNA

I doubt we'll be staying that long.

They stand, awkwardly.

ANGIE remains positive and diplomatically changes subject.

ANGIE

Where's Ben?

DONNA

Trying to find a park out on the street.

ANGIE

Surely he knows he can park his car in my driveway?

DONNA gives withering look.

DONNA

I think there's been more than enough of that sort of talk already.

ANGIE

I know this must be a difficult time for you.

DONNA

The only difficult thing is your dippy hippy ideas and the harm they're causing.

ANGIE

You've always respected my beliefs in the past.

DONNA

In the past, they've been harmless.

RICHARD enters, sad and broken.

RICHARD

Donna. I'm so glad you could make it.

RICHARD hugs DONNA, lingering into a distraught embrace.

Unsure, DONNA gives him a light pat on his back.

DONNA

It'll be okay, Rich.

RICHARD disengages and composes himself.

RICHARD

Sorry. This must be just as hard for you.

DONNA

Not quite.

RICHARD

You're just as much a victim here as me.

DONNA

We're not victims. We're pissing about giving credence to new age twaddle.

RICHARD

You're in the denial stage, I can tell.

SOUND FX: Front door closes.

BEN enters with a noticeable black eye and sticking plaster on face.

A tension between the two men.

RICHARD offers hand begrudgingly.

RICHARD

Benjamin.

BEN flinches at the movement, then shakes hands cautiously.

BEN

Richard.

Awkward silence.

ANGIE

That eye is starting to look better.

BEN glares at RICHARD.

BEN

Yes, the swelling is almost gone.

RICHARD

No hard feelings, Ben?

BEN

It took two days to regain any feeling, actually.

DONNA

Is the psycho-hypno-whatever-she-is here? I want to get this over with.

ANGIE

Tess is preparing some nibblies.

DONNA

So how do we do this? Sit round a campfire with our feet in hummus chanting "Omm" until you finally apologise?

ANGIE

It's a little more scientific than that, Donna. I hope you'll treat this situation with the respect it deserves.

DONNA

I already am.

ANGIE

Richard, if you could help fetch the seating.

ANGIE departs OFF.

RICHARD lays comforting hand on DONNA's shoulder.

ANGIE calls sharply from OFF-STAGE.

ANGIE

Richard!

RICHARD scoots OFF obediently.

DONNA

First sign of incense and a goat, we're out of

here.

BEN

Clearing the air is the only way to sort all this out.

TESS enters with BOWL of nibbles, which BEN takes automatically.

BEN

Cheers. Just two coffees, thanks.

TESS

Excuse me?

BEN frowns in recognition.

BEN

Sorry, I thought you were a waitress.

TESS

In your friend's house?

BEN

… yeah.

TESS

Interesting.

TESS takes out NOTEPAD and PEN, jots her thoughts.

DONNA

Are you the hypnotherapist?

TESS

Among my professional services. You must be
Ben and … *(consults NOTEPAD)* Donna?

BEN clutches DONNA in a gruff show of togetherness.

BEN

That's right. This is Donna. The love of my life.

TESS looks at BEN, then jots again in NOTEPAD.

*BEN and DONNA lean forwards to peek – quickly back as TESS
finishes.*

TESS gives BEN an appraising look up and down.

TESS

I've heard a lot about *you*, Ben.

BEN

Well, not me, exactly.

TESS

Yes, I told Angela you'd be defensive.

DONNA

So, you're the person filling Angie's head with this
rubbish?

TESS

I'm simply a facilitator, allowing my clients to
experience the full extent of *all* life experiences.

My card.

TESS hands them BUSINESS CARDS each.

DONNA

(Reads) Qualified Alternative Cognitive Consultant. "Quack". How appropriate.

DONNA gives CARD back, TESS checks it with dismay. BEN pockets his CARD.

ANGIE and RICHARD return with five ornate CUSHIONS.

RICHARD gives DONNA a CUSHION, then thrusts CUSHION roughly into BEN's midriff.

ANGIE

You've met Tess, my therapist?

TESS

Not the waitress.

ANGIE

What?

BEN

I just confused Tess with a café waitress I saw once. … And a bar maid.

All look to BEN.

TESS

So, you see me in some sort of on-going service menial motif?

BEN

No. Just mistaken identity, I guess.

TESS

Mmm.

TESS jots again in NOTEPAD.

BEN

What are you writing?

TESS

Not your order.

ANGIE

Maybe we should begin?

ANGIE hands a CUSHION to TESS.

They place CUSHIONS on floor in a shallow arc: TESS centre, ANGIE and DONNA at her sides, RICHARD and BEN at ends.

They sit, TESS, ANGIE and RICHARD cross-legged, so BEN and DONNA follow their lead.

TESS

Besides Angela, has anyone else here undergone

or witnessed hypnotherapeutic regression?

DONNA raises hand.

DONNA

I once went to the circus and watched the clowns. Does that count?

TESS

This will work much better with open minds.

DONNA

If not completely vacant ones.

BEN

Remember what I said, Donna.

RICHARD

Yet you don't seem to remember what you've done.

BEN

I didn't do anything!

RICHARD

Angela seems pretty sure you *did* her!

TESS

I don't think this is particularly constructive interplay.

DONNA

What is all this meant to prove?

ANGIE

Since neither you nor Ben believe me, I thought if I underwent regression with you here, it would help us better understand the situation we find ourselves in.

BEN

What, here? Now? In front of Richard?

RICHARD adopts a serene half-lotus pose.

RICHARD

I'm perfectly fine with the idea, Ben.

BEN

No, you're bloody not! You clocked me over it just last Wednesday.

RICHARD

I was angry then. Emotions were raw and fresh.

BEN

And they'll be a damn sight fresher if we go through with this!

RICHARD

So, you admit something happened!

DONNA

He doesn't admit anything!

ANGIE

By facing this through, we can all sort out our

feelings and move on.

DONNA

That'll only happen when you drop this, and we forget it ever happened – which it didn't – ASAP!

BEN

Whatever sorts this out so we can all just go back to being friends.

RICHARD

(Sotto) Who sleep with the other's partners.

DONNA

What?

RICHARD

Nothing.

TESS

I'm sensing some tension here.

DONNA

Wow. You're good.

TESS

This won't work unless we're all relaxed and conducive to the process.

ANGIE

I think we should hold hands, take a deep breath, then exhale as one.

DONNA

(Taps BEN's shoulder) Wake me up when the performing monkeys come on.

ANGIE and TESS join hands, BEN and RICHARD comply, DONNA begrudgingly.

TESS

And in on three. One. Two.

They breathe in.

TESS

And hold. … then out.

They breathe out.

DONNA

(On breath) Nutters.

TESS

I shall now induce Angela into a relaxed hypnotic state, then we'll proceed into regression.

BEN

Do you use a swinging watch or something?

TESS

This isn't some conjuring trick, Ben. Besides, she's already under.

They realise ANGIE is immobile, eyes closed.

RICHARD

Wow, that's amazing.

DONNA rolls her head back in disbelief.

TESS

She's had so many sessions now, it hardly takes any effort at all.

RICHARD reacts, BEN shifts uneasily.

DONNA

How do we know she's under? She could be faking.

ANGIE

I am not faking.

DONNA

She's listening!

TESS

Even under hypnosis, the patient is still aware of the environment and things we say.

DONNA

(Sotto) Faker.

ANGIE

I heard that!

DONNA

Just testing.

TESS

Please, Angela, concentrate. Now, where are you?

ANGIE

I'm … on the farm.

RICHARD

(Immediately furious) Is this *the* farm? Where *he* is?

TESS

Ssh. Now Angie, where on the farm are you?

ANGIE

I'm alone, in the barn.

BEN

The barn again? I'll need my antihistamines.
(Notices RICHARD's reaction) Sorry.

ANGIE

But I'm not alone. *He's* here. Ben, his former self.
He's just entering.

RICHARD

He's *what?*

ANGIE

The barn. He moves silently in through the
doors, careful not to make a sound and wake the
homestead.

RICHARD

Clever. Sneaky and clever.

BEN

It's not me!

ANGIE

We've only moonlight to see. I see him gazing at me. *Wanting* me.

DONNA

Oh, good grief.

TESS

Is this one of the occasions we've gone through before?

ANGIE

No, this is a different one.

TESS

Another one?

RICHARD

Another one!

TESS

Ssh. What's happening, Angela?

ANGIE

He's lifting up his shirt, revealing a smooth muscled chest.

DONNA

You've been working out. And waxing.

ANGIE

He sweeps me up in his arms, holding me close.

RICHARD

How close?

ANGIE

So close I can hear his heart beating, pounding in time with mine.

Flushed by the racy details, TESS fans herself with her NOTEPAD.

DONNA

Has she been reading Mills and Boon lately?

RICHARD

(Gritted teeth) And what does he do next?

TESS

Don't rush her.

ANGIE

He kisses me. Long, passionately, deeply.

RICHARD

Does he now!

BEN

I'm not doing a thing!

DONNA

It can't be Ben. We never kiss like that.

ANGIE

Then he gazes into my eyes, stroking my cheek.
Lightly with the barest touch of his fingers.

TESS fans herself a little quicker.

DONNA

Hang on, you do that now.

BEN

Coincidence.

RICHARD

Trespass.

ANGIE

Touching my cheek, he kisses me again, then
slides his mouth to my ear, whispering my name.
One, twice, over and over.

DONNA sits up, this is too close to home.

BEN

Coincidence!

ANGIE

(Impassioned throes) Suddenly, we can't help
ourselves!

All are startled by ANGIE's sudden intensity.

ANGIE

He removes my dress urgently, hands freeing my body! He kisses my bare shoulders, lips running up my neck as he runs his hands down the curves of my waist!

TESS

Here we go again.

DONNA

Did you tell her about last Tuesday?

BEN

Of course not!

DONNA

They're the same moves you pulled on me!

RICHARD

Moves on my wife!

BEN

It's not real!

ANGIE

The barn whirls like a dream, but it is real. You unhook my brassiere, freeing me.

RICHARD

No!

BEN

(To RICHARD) No!

ANGIE

You clasp me close, skin to skin, kissing. You tell me I'm your everything.

DONNA

She's your everything?

BEN

She's not.

ANGIE

"You are", you moan.

RICHARD

You bastard!

RICHARD stands, rolling up sleeves.

RICHARD

Right, put me under. I'm going in there to sort this out right here and now.

TESS

You can't, it's a memory!

RICHARD

Right there and then, then!

BEN

It's memory! Past. Implanted. Not real. Not now,

not happening, not cheating!

RICHARD sits, not satisfied.

TESS

Actually, the experience of the memory is now, so technically it is happening.

BEN

You keep out of it. *(To RICHARD)* You're wrong!

ANGIE

It's wrong, we know. How can this be right, I say.

BEN

Now you start asking.

ANGIE

But as you lay me down in the hay –

BEN sneezes. DONNA glares in suspicion.

ANGIE

… I know this can only be pure and true.

BEN

It's not true!

RICHARD

Some friend I thought you were!

BEN

It's just fantasy.

ANGIE

– you say, but as I watch you slowly undress, we know this fantasy can only be true.

DONNA

If she mentions your birthmark …

RICHARD

(Urgent to ANGIE) Is there a birthmark?

BEN

There won't be a birthmark!

ANGIE

I gasp.

TESS, RICHARD, BEN, DONNA gasp, holding their breath.

ANGIE

But the noise is only some cattle nearby.

TESS

And out.

All breathe out.

ANGIE

My breath comes in pants as you lay atop me.

DONNA

A shame you couldn't keep it in your pants!

RICHARD

Is there a birthmark?!

ANGIE

You kiss your way up my body.

DONNA

You better skip the navel.

ANGIE

You circle my navel with soft kisses.

DONNA

Bastard.

ANGIE

A hundred light sweet kisses up my torso, with haphazard but intentional detours.

RICHARD

What sort of detours?

TESS

(Fanning with gusto) Never mind the detours!

RICHARD

What sort of detours?

ANGIE

Now you're kissing me. Wholly. Completely.

Totally.

RICHARD

No!

ANGIE

Yes!

DONNA

You never kiss me wholly and completely.

BEN

I do!

RICHARD

How could you?

BEN

I didn't!

ANGIE

We're out of control!

RICHARD leaps up to assault BEN.

RICHARD

Come here!

BEN commando rolls to his feet, holding CUSHION as a shield. DONNA is in tears.

TESS blocks RICHARD's path, swotting him back with

NOTEPAD.

TESS

Not now! She's getting to the good bits!

DONNA

I can't hear any more!

DONNA runs OFF in tears.

RICHARD slips past TESS. BEN pushes CUSHION into RICHARD, then rushes OFF.

RICHARD gives chase.

ANGIE

Passionately, rhythmically, moving as one! Hearts beating, arms, legs, bodies entwined! Like cold white stallion and mare in the moonlight, manes billowing, our love galloping free across the hills in the cool dark night.

Unsure, TESS taps ANGIE on shoulder. ANGIE comes to.

TESS

You *haven't* been reading Mills and Boon lately, have you?

SCENE FOUR – CAFÉ

The MANTELPIECE is transformed back to the café COUNTER with COFFEE MACHINE.

TABLE with two CHAIRS are replaced as per the opening scene.

LIGHTS – SPOT on BEN at TABLE.

BEN sits alone, MOBILE to ear. He sits up as the line connects.

BEN

Donna?

He sinks in dismay – it's only her voicemail.

BEN

Donna, I'm leaving another message because –
… Please. This is stupid. *(Corrects)* Not your
reaction, or your hurt feelings. I mean, the
situation. … Please call me. Please.

LIGHTS UP as …

… WAITRESS serves a COFFEE to BEN.

BEN reaches for wallet.

WAITRESS

No, no. On the house. You look like you need it.

WAITRESS returns to COUNTER.

BEN is still bemused by her likeness to Tess.

Reminded, BEN takes out BUSINESS CARD and dials on MOBILE then rings. He turns, back to the "door".

BEN

Hello? Tess? This is Ben, your client Angie's … friend. … Yes, that Ben. … No, Donna's still not talking to me.

As BEN speaks, RICHARD enters and looks around.

WAITRESS points to BEN.

RICHARD nods thanks and sits. BEN doesn't notice.

BEN

Look, could I book a session with you? … No, not to find any of my past lives. I'm rather hoping we might get this one back.

Frowning, RICHARD looks back at WAITRESS, vaguely recognising her, but decides he must be mistaken.

BEN

Tuesday? Great.

BEN ends the call then is startled to see RICHARD sitting opposite.

BEN

(Wary) Richard.

RICHARD nods an awkward manly greeting.

RICHARD

Benjamin.

They sit in silence.

BEN grows unsure as RICHARD slowly builds to speak.

RICHARD

… How's it going?

BEN

I've had better days. And lives, apparently.

RICHARD slowly builds to speak again.

RICHARD

… I've been giving the situation some thought. Now, I'm not saying I jumped to any conclusions in all this. But there may have been some … *over-reactions* the other night.

BEN

(Crosses arms, unimpressed) Really.

RICHARD

(Glare) Maybe. … There's been some damage done. Sorting it out won't be easy.

BEN

No, it won't.

They sit with manly pouts.

RICHARD brings himself to speak again.

RICHARD

I … went and did one of those hypnotic
regressions. To understand it better. See what it's
all about for myself.

BEN

It's a load of old nonsense, isn't it.

*RICHARD initially chuckles along with BEN, then slowly fades into
a non-committal shrug.*

RICHARD

We regressed me to a past life. To see if I figured
as a piece of Angie's puzzle.

BEN

And did you?

RICHARD

Nah, not me. What would I be doing on a farm?

BEN chuckles, tension easing.

*RICHARD sees BEN chuckling, so chuckles too, though not totally
aware of what about. He grows troubled again.*

RICHARD

It was one of my other lives though, that was the thing. … Bit of a concern.

Tenderly, RICHARD places his hand on BEN's knee.

RICHARD

Ben, mate. We've got some explaining to do.

END

72

Principle Props

- A bench that can resemble a Café COUNTER, a public BAR, and a living room MANTELPIECE

Café

- An object resembling a Café COFFEE MACHINE

- A "STEAMER" to spurt "steam" on cue

- BOWL OF MUFFINS

- Two Café TABLES with easy-to-move CHAIRS

- STOOLS at the COUNTER

- CUPS with SAUCERS and SPOONS. One cup needs liquid for Ben to spit out

- NAPKINS and other Café ephemera

- CHOCOLATE SHAKER for making cappuccinos

- CLEANING CLOTH for "polishing" and WASHCLOTH for wiping up liquid

- Angie wears a WATCH

- Ben has a MOBILE PHONE in Scene 4

Bar

- BEER TAPS or nearest facsimile

- PINT GLASSES with liquid

- CREDIT CARD

- Cardboard BAR MATS

- TOWEL

- BROOM

Living Room

- ORNAMENTS, FRAMED PHOTOS

- FIREPLACE GRILLE

- BOWL of nibbles
- NOTEPAD and PEN
- BUSINESS CARDS
- Five large CUSHIONS

About the Author

Martin Lindsay is a Western Australian writer hidden away in the leafy seaside town of Dunsborough.

He is the author of the plays *Spd D8n*, *One Night One Day* and *Brown Acid*, and award-winning one-act plays *One Night Stand Off* and *Past Loves*.

Other plays include one-act *Someone Called Rob*, and finalists in the Short + Sweet and Arkfest ten-minute play festivals with *Couch*, *The Retirement Gift*, *That Little Voice*, and *Possum Play*.

Martin was a contributing writer for *Lifted* in the 2013 Perth Fringe Festival, and co-wrote and directed the comedy monologue/burlesque *Lock-In Love* for the 2014 Adelaide Fringe Festival and 2014 Melbourne Comedy Festival.

Martin's short stories have been included in Black Inc's *Best Australian Stories 2012*, and won the 2013 Stringybark Humorous Short Story Competition, the 2014 Joe O'Sullivan Writers Prize, and the 2019 Peter Cowan Short Story award. His micro-fiction has appeared in Short and Twisted editions and Night Parrot Press' *Once* (2020), *Twice Not Shy* (2021), and *Three Can Keep a Secret* (2022) collections.

He is even known to occasionally blog on his website at martinlindsay.net, when not trying to stop parrots from having sex on his balcony railing.

Martin's debut novel *Wil, Maree and the Mattress* will be available soon from Moody Lapcat Books.

Plays by the Same Author

- Spd D8n

- Someone Called Rob

- One Night One Day

- Brown Acid

- Couch

- Framed

- The Retirement Gift

- That Little Voice

- Possum Play

- Third Date's the Charm

Spd D8n

A play in two acts by Martin Lindsay

At a speed dating evening at a local pub, five singles consider the question – How much can you really learn about someone in four minutes?

Ahead of them is a night of hope, hell, and free Cosmopolitans.

And maybe the chance to find what they didn't know they were looking for.

*"Hang on. I'm not **quite** drunk enough to make it to the end of your story."*

"How did you get into that line of work? Did you not study or something?"

"That possibly came across as a bit needy."

"Polyamory sounds an awful lot like just rootin' around."

"They call me Mike. Rhymes with bike. Maybe you can ride me sometime."

Available now from Moody Lapcat Books.

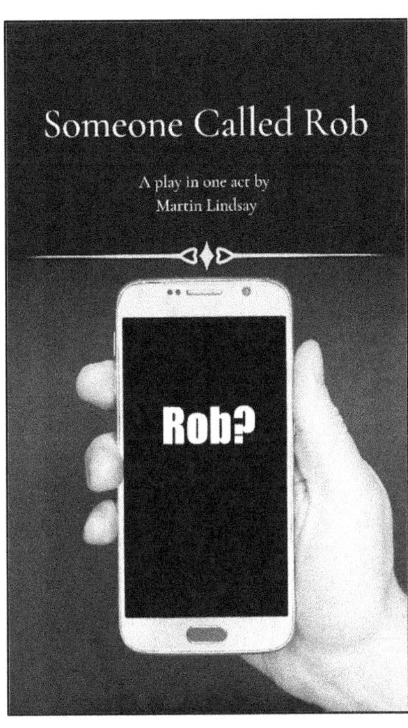

Someone Called Rob

A play in one act by Martin Lindsay

Sometimes it pays to just let the call go through to voicemail...

Rob answers an unknown caller on his mobile.

An angry guy called Adam reveals just what Rob did last night. That's why Adam is angry.

And *everyone* knows what happens when Adam gets angry.

And Adam has Rob's phone number...

As Rob learns, a lot can be discovered from just a phone number.

Available now from Moody Lapcat Books.

One Night One Day

A play in two acts by Martin Lindsay

A comedy about singles and social graces, after a night that went so right goes so wrong the next morning.

Rachel and Greg wake up together after a night out on the town, much to the surprise of both.

An awkward situation at the best of times, made all the more awkward as details from the previous night slowly filter back to them…

Coming soon from Moody Lapcat Books.

Brown Acid

**A play in two acts by
Martin Lindsay**

Throughout rock'n'roll history, from small beginnings sometimes legendary bands grow...

And sometimes, they don't.

Wanted:

Musicians to join original four-piece rock band.

Serious gigging opportunities with a group that is going places. Own transport would suit.

NO TIME WASTERS!

Coming soon from Moody Lapcat Books.

Moody Lapcat Books

Books better than belly rubs

Moody Lapcat Books is an independent publisher of books and plays.

Visit moodylapcatbooks.com to see our latest releases, things to come, or enquire about performance rights.

Or contact@moodylapcatbooks.com